Participant Manual
Lasting Love

Skills to a Better Relationship

(Your Name)

Table of Contents

Introduction

10 Rules for a Healthy Marriage

1. Never hit, threaten, intimidate, or demean your partner

2. Practice fidelity

3. Never take your partner for granted

4. Remember the little things

5. Practice forgiveness and learn to apologize

6. Never go to bed angry

7. Never miss a chance to say "I love you"

8. Say something supportive of your partner daily

9. Never insult your partner

10. Touch daily

Section | 1
Communication Skills

Exercise 1.1: Listen Up

• First, don't talk until you know you have 100 percent of your partner's attention. Tell your partner:

> **"This issue is really important to me."**

• Second, the listener must learn how to focus all attention on the speaker. The listener must put aside whatever else s/he is doing. Put other thoughts out of mind.

• Third, the listener must repeat what he s/he thinks the speaker said and meant.

• Fourth, the speaker has to confirm that the listener understood the point.

Now, to make sure that everyone follows the rules, no one may speak, unless s/he has the "microphone."

While s/he is holding the "microphone," only s/he can talk. When it is time to respond, the partner takes the "mic" and only the partner can talk.

Remember, this technique is not effective if you overuse it. If everything you say is important, then nothing is important.

What is important to your partner may not be important to you. Learning to listen will help your relationship because it will force you to pay attention to the issues that your partner feels are important. This skill will help your partner pay attention to issues that are important to you.

Notes: Practice: Listen up

Exercise 1.2: It's Communicating the Little Things

Marriage is made up of thousand and thousands of little events. The way we learn to communicate and deal with all the little things determines the quality of our relationship or marriage.

It is what is important to your partner that counts, not what you think should be important.

Notes: What are the "little things" you like about your partner?

Demonstration

• Make a list of 5 little things that your partner does that drive you crazy or annoy you. We are not talking about appearance, but behavior. <u>Do not show your partner your list</u>.

• Now, tell your partner just one of these five things. Do this in just 60 seconds. Tell your partner that you know this is a little thing, but that it bothers you and is important to you.

• Ask your partner if s/he will change just this one thing. <u>Don't criticize</u>. The point is to try to get your partner to change behavior by communicating more effectively.

• Partner, make a commitment to change just this one small thing. Don't be defensive. It isn't time to defend your behavior but to commit to changing it because it's important to your partner.

Section One Homework

Participants should practice this exercise every day for three weeks.

1. Speaker: identify an issue that is really important to you. Tell your partner how important the issue is and ask for 100% of their attention. Listener: Make sure you are focusing all of your attention on your partner.

2. After the speaker has finished, the listener must repeat what they think their partner said and meant.

3. The speaker now confirms that the listener understood the point.

After the three weeks, sit down and talk to your partner about how this is working. Discuss what you have learned.

Has this exercise led to any changes in behavior?

Has it led to any changes in feelings?

After three weeks, you should automatically start using these skills. If not, go back to practicing the exercise twice a week for another three weeks.

Notes

Notes

Section|2
Conflict Resolution

Skill Building Session Two

Abuse can take different forms.

The most serious is physical abuse. Physical abuse is illegal, as well as destructive, and should not be tolerated.

If your partner begins to physically abuse you, you must seek professional help.

The chances are, it will get worse, not better.

But there are other forms of abusive behavior, too: demeaning insults, intimidation, screaming, yelling, and destroying property.

These forms of abuse can be just as destructive in themselves and can lead to worse abuse, even escalating into violence, especially when the person is under the influence of drugs or alcohol, or is under increased pressure at work or at home.

For most people, learning a set of skills to help control your emotions.

 Exercise 2.1: Back Off And Talk (BOAT)

Notes: What happens when we are abused, scream at, threaten, or hit our partner?

How do we Deal with this Anger and Emotion?
BOAT. It stands for Back Off And Talk.

• Back off at the very first sign of anger. It is the most important step you can take.

• Move back 5 steps. Only when you back away, can you begin to control your own aggressive emotions. Only when you physically back away, can your partner stop feeling threatened by you.

• Sit Down. We stop threatening when we make ourselves smaller.

• Talk. Don't raise your voice, but tell your partner what it is you are feeling in a normal tone of voice, like asking for a cup of coffee.

Exercise 2.2: Count to Ten

The fourth step in BOAT is to talk.

In order for this technique to work, you must learn how to relax.

But if you start talking before you've changed your feelings, the talking may escalate into yelling or worse.

Here is what you need to do to reduce anger immediately.

> **Notes: What are some of the places you can think of that might relax you?**

• **Take five deep breaths. Before you say a word, breathe.**

• **Close your eyes and imagine you are in the most relaxing place you can think of. This can be any place but really bring it up in detail on the spot.**

• **While you are in your relaxation space mentally, take 5 more deep breathes. Very slowly breathe in, then slowly exhale.**

If we have done this well, we will have reduced or eliminated the very chemicals that make us feel angry and allow us to abuse the people we love the most.

Only now can we begin to talk. After telling our partner that we are no longer angry, we can quietly say why we were getting angry.

It is very important to understand how important "tone of voice" is to reassure our partner that we are no longer threatening.

OK, now do this exercise with your partner. Remember one thing that your partner does that makes you angry. But before you speak, breathe slowly, and think of your relaxation space. Only after you've done this, begin speaking in a normal voice. Use the same tone of voice you'd use to say "Pass me the salt," or "The coffee's ready."

Notes

Exercise 2.3: Words Matter

We've all heard the saying that goes, "Sticks and stones may break my bones, but words can never hurt me." Well, it's just not true. Words can hurt. They can leave scars almost as deep as real, physical ones.

How many of you can remember something someone you love once said to you that hurt you deeply?

Most of us have either said hurtful things or had them said to us. We often remember something cruel said to us years, even decades later.

Notes: We can hurt our partners with words. What are the kinds of things we should never say to our partner?

• **Words can scar as deeply as actual wounds, so choose your words carefully. You're more likely to get through to him/her if you choose a constructive way to pass on negative information.**

Three benefits of practicing BOAT

Homework

• Make a list of the 5 things that trigger your anger. Share with your partner. These should not be minor annoyances, but the type of things that might make you lose control.

• Pick one item from your list. You can go through the list over time, but don't try to do everything at once.

• Using the techniques you practiced last week (Listen Up) tell your partner one thing s/he says or does that makes you angry. Make sure you do this in a conversational voice.

• Using the techniques you practiced last week, let your partner respond by saying what s/he heard you say and s/he thinks you meant.

• Now tell your partner what you experienced as you hear him or her talk.

Section | 3
Practicing Fidelity

Improve Your Sex Life and Stay Faithful

For Men Only (women on page 26)

Skill Building Session Three

A few simple rules to help you have a good romantic life.

1. **Commit to Fidelity**

2. **Avoid temptation**

3. **Focus your sexual energy on your partner**

4. **Communicate clearly about sex**

5. **Be as appealing as you can**

Exercise 3.1: Avoiding Temptation

What are the ways we avoid temptation?

Avoid Going to Bars and Parties alone

Don't use the internet chat rooms or personals

Don't go to lunch or dinner alone with other women

OTHERS:

Exercise 3.2: Focusing All Your Sexual Energy on Your Partner

Part of "practicing fidelity" is about turning our partners into the sole objects of our sexual desire.

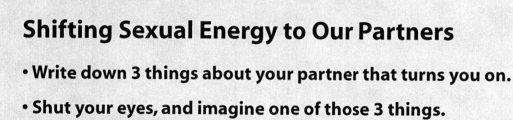

Shifting Sexual Energy to Our Partners

• Write down 3 things about your partner that turns you on.

• Shut your eyes, and imagine one of those 3 things.

• Now imagine another one.

Do this once a day for two weeks.

Communicate Clearly about Sex

Not knowing whether your partner is willing to make love, even if she may not desire it on her own, discourages some men from initiating lovemaking.

How do you tell your partner that you are not interested?
And how do you communicate "availability"?

One of the most important things you can do to improve your sex life is to learn how to communicate more clearly:

❏ **YES**   ❏ **NO**   ❏ **AVAILABLE**

Sometimes, there are good reasons why your partner may not want to make love and this does not mean that she desires you less or doesn't love you.

What are the reasons your partner may not want to make love tonight?

	Others
She is sick	
Anxious	
Tired	
We had sex recently	
My hygiene	

Do you feel that your partner or wife effectively tells you why she doesn't want to make love? **Never let sex be a chore for your wife or partner.**

This is a very hard for us men to understand. Men want sex when they want it and expect their partners to have the same needs, or at least to accommodate their needs.

Having a good sex life requires us to be able to understand when our wives and partners want sex and when they don't.

Exercise 3.3: Communicating Clearly About Sex

How do I know when my partner wants to make love?

This question has three possible answers.

Yes

No

Available

This third category is often the key to a good sex life.

When is your partner willing or available for sex even
though she may not be planning to make love? And how do you know?

• **Write down ways you know your partner definitely wants to make love.**

• **Write how you know your partner is definitely not interested in lovemaking.**

• **Write down how you know that your partner is available.**

Notes:

How do you communicate with your partner that you want to make love?

Imagine your wife or partner walking in the door, she is exhausted from a hard day at work. She thinks to herself: "I have to change clothes, cook dinner, clean up after, check the homework, make sure the kids have clean clothes for tomorrow, then take care of Alfred's needs." It doesn't sound like much fun.

For some people, it is easier to just make a regular time to have sex.

But you can have sex more often than your planned date, but setting a time when you regularly have sex can take the anxiety out of wondering whether your partner is available. If you are going to take this approach, it is important that you talk about it. Think of it as a "date" and agree on a time in advance.

This should not stop you from being spontaneous and having sex more frequently. But it will take the tension out of deciding.

Exercise 3.4: Making Yourself Appealing

Men are encouraged in our culture to think their partners should look like movie stars.

But just because we can't all look like stars doesn't mean we have to look like slobs either. Part of keeping romance alive in a relationship is working to be as appealing as possible, even if we will never win any beauty contests.

• **Write down three things you can do to make yourself more appealing**

Notes

• **Decide on one short-term goal and put it into action immediately (This can be something as simple as putting on a clean shirt and pants when you come home from work instead of a torn t-shirt and sweats)**

• **Decide on one long-term goal and stick with it)**

Homework

• **Discuss with your partner the three options for lovemaking: yes, no, available**

• **Decide with each other how you will communicate these three options**

• **Come up with a simple signal that you will use to telegraph these three options possibilities (Remember, these don't have to be words, but could be a bedtime routine like showering right before bed or wearing something special to bed. The important thing is to decide how you will communicate and then be consistent.)**

Improve Your Sex Life and Stay Faithful

For Women Only (men on page 20)

Skill Building Session Three

How many marriages and relationships break up over sex? Infidelity is the top reason couples give for divorce.

Fidelity is not just an old-fashioned idea. It is the only way to guarantee that you have a secure, loving relationship. It is the way we have complete trust in our partners.

The first step to staying faithful is to be committed to having the best sex you possibly can with your partner.

We are going to give you a few simple rules and teach you a few skills to help you have a good romantic life.

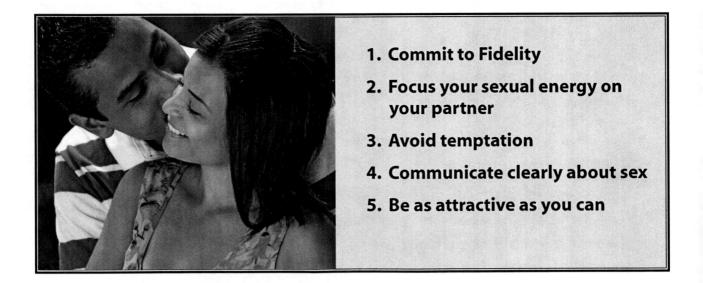

1. **Commit to Fidelity**
2. **Focus your sexual energy on your partner**
3. **Avoid temptation**
4. **Communicate clearly about sex**
5. **Be as attractive as you can**

Exercise 3.1: Focusing Sexual Energy on Your Partner

When you are thinking romantically, whose picture comes to mind? Do you sometimes fantasize about men at work? The latest American Idol? Will Smith? Leonardo DiCaprio? How many of you can honestly say that when the idea of romance comes into your head, it's your husband or boyfriend whose face and body naturally come to mind?

One of the most important ways to avoid infidelity is to concentrate those romantic and erotic fantasies on our partners. But how do we do that? How do we focus all our sexual attention on our partners?

- **Write down 3 things about your partner that turn you on.**

- **Shut your eyes, and imagine one of those 3 things.**

- **Now imagine another one.**

Men and women are different. The things that arouse you may not be the same as those that arouse your partner. Men are far more likely to be turned on by pictures, sexy clothes, anything that directly signals sex. Women often focus more on romance than sex. We need to feel romantic before we feel desire.

The important thing is to know what it is that puts you in the proper mood to make love and to be able to communicate your desire or receptivity to your partner.

Notes: What are some of the things that put you in aromantic/erotic mood?

Exercise 3.2: Communicating Clearly About Sex

REMEMBER COMMUNICATIONS SKILLS

Do I know when my partner wants to make love?

This question has three possible answers.

What are they?

Yes

No

Available

This third category is often the key to a good sex life. When are we willing or available for sex even though we may not be planning to make love.

We need to let our partner know that we are interested, definitely not interested, or weren't necessarily thinking about it but might be open to lovemaking anyway.

How do you tell your partner: "I need you to hold me, but I don't want to have sex."

- **Write how you know your partner is interested in lovemaking.**
- **Write down how you communicate "yes," you're definitely interested.**
- **Write how you communicate "no" you're definitely not interested**
- **Write down how you can communicate "available."**

Homework

Let your partner know, every day for the next two weeks when you are:

• **Available**

• **Want to make love**

• **Do not want to make love**

Notes: What are some reasons you might not want to have sex?

You need to make sure that your partner understands these reasons. If he knows that you do not want to have sex when you are exhausted or when you have to wake up early the next morning, then he will understand better when you say no.

If you're definitely not in the mood, how can you communicate "no" without it being hurtful and rejecting?

Notes: What are the wrong ways to say no?

Date Night

Another approach that will help avoid conflict over when you have sex is to talk about it and agree on a date and time in advance. For example, if you are sure you will have sex once a week, agree that Friday or Saturday night, or perhaps Saturday morning, is your "date" time.

Notes: What are the things we can say or do after sex?

Exercise 3.3: Avoiding Temptation

Men need sex for a physical outlet. So you need to be aware of your man's timetable.

Most men want sex more than women.

This has been the case forever.

But now things have changed. Fidelity is harder than ever.

How have things changed?

Values have changed.

Sex is everywhere–temptation is way up.

Internet makes meeting women easier than ever.

There are more single women than eligible single men.

More single women are willing to have sex with married men.

TV shows applaud sex outside of marriage.

The stigma against infidelity is gone. Few are willing to say: "Infidelity is wrong."

Does that mean all men are going to be unfaithful?

No. It means women have to communicate better than ever and be committed to having a good sex life.

It means women need to be aware of the sexual needs of our men, and aware of the temptations that men face.

But men aren't the only ones who face temptation.

We also need to be aware of the temptations women face.

How many of you meet men at work who you are attracted to?

And do you socialize outside of work with any of these men?

How many of you have met men on the Internet?

How about chat rooms?

How do we avoid temptation?

Don't fantasize about other men. Fantasize about partner.

Avoid situations which will tempt you.

Don't go to parties without your husband.

Do not use the Internet to meet men.

Do not go to chat rooms for singles.

Focus all your sexual energy on your husband or boyfriend.

Make him the object of all your sexual attention.

This will help us be faithful. And it will help our men be faithful.

No one wants their partner to be unfaithful. But we often do not work hard enough at having a good sex life.

Exercise 3.4: Making Yourself Appealing

Men and women are encouraged in our culture to think their partners should look like movie stars. But this is both unrealistic and destructive. Men and women should try to be as appealing as possible, even if we are not movie stars.

Notes: So how do we work at being appealing?

You are as sexy as you feel and as sexy as you act.

Since these assignments are designed to improve your love life, you should be motivated to do them.

• **Write down three things you can do to make yourself more appealing.**

• **Decide on one short-term goal and put it into action immediately. (This can be something as simple as putting on a clean shirt and pants when you come home from work instead of a torn t-shirt and sweats.)**

• **Decide on one long-term goal and stick with it. Start exercising —and try doing it together.**

Homework

• **Discuss with your partner the three options for lovemaking: yes, no, available.**

• **Decide how you will communicate with each other these three.**

• **Come up with a simple signal that you will use to telegraph these three options possibilities** (Remember, these don't have to be words, but could be a bedtime routine like showering right before bed or wearing something special to bed. The important thing is to decide how you will communicate and then be consistent.)

Notes

Section | 4
Financial Skills

Skill Building Session Four

Most couples don't always agree on how to spend your money. And you don't talk about it until it's too late.

Exercise 4.1: Money Talks.

Write down the answers to the following questions. Don't show the answers to your partners yet.

- Have you set financial goals? ❑ YES ❑ NO

- Do you agree on your financial goals? ❑ YES ❑ NO

- Do you agree on priorities for household purchases? ❑ YES ❑ NO

- Do you have a plan for saving to purchase a home? ❑ YES ❑ NO

- Do you think your partner spends too much money on clothes? ❑ YES ❑ NO

- Too much on entertainment? ❑ YES ❑ NO

- Does your partner gamble? ❑ YES ❑ NO

- Does your partner spend money on drinking or drugs? ❑ YES ❑ NO

- Extravagant gifts? ❑ YES ❑ NO

- Cars? ❑ YES ❑ NO

- Does your partner hide his or her spending from you? ❑ YES ❑ NO

- Does your partner buy things on the internet without your knowing? ❑ YES ❑ NO

- Do you carry credit card debt? ❑ YES ❑ NO

- Does your partner jeopardize your security with her or his spending? ❑ YES ❑ NO

The first step is to decide what your goals are. Discuss your top three financial goals for the next year. Then set up a plan on how you're going to achieve those goals.

• **Write down the answer to each of the questions. Make sure your partner doesn't see your answers.**

• **Compare your answers with your partner's answers.**

• **Talk about it. Where do you agree? Where are the biggest disagreements?**

• **Set goals. Pick one financial goal that you can both agree to. This should be something that is achievable in a reasonable time frame.**

• **Make a plan. Decide what steps you are going to take to reach your goal and set up some benchmarks that you can monitor to achieve your goal.**

Notes: What are some important financial goals you have?

Exercise 4.2: Obstacles to Achieving Financial Goals

Notes: Why do our financial plans can go awry?

Here are some tips to help you avoid the pitfalls:

• <u>Talk about spending</u>. Agree on priorities and what you will each spend money on. Take time once a week to talk about your spending for the past week and the coming week.

• <u>Make a budget and live within your budget</u>. This includes a budget for gifts for each other and gifts for your children.

• <u>No surprises</u>. Do not go out and spend money that you have not agreed to.

• <u>Consider ways to save money, even when you have to spend it</u>. When you are on a tight budget, it's important to look for ways to pay less than full retail. Decide to buy only when things are on sale. Look around for the best deal; comparison shopping can save you money. Buy used products when you can: cars, furniture, electronics, even clothes. The minute you drive away from the dealership, your "new" car is worth thousands of dollars less than the sticker price—and a fraction of what you'll pay over the life of the loan.

• <u>If you don't own a home, you shouldn't be buying fancy jewelry, cars, and electronic equipment</u>. Owning your own home represents financial security for you and your family. If you don't have security, you can't afford luxuries. Until you own your own home and can live within your budget, avoid wasteful spending.

• <u>Avoid buying things online or from the shopping networks on TV</u>. These items sometimes look like a bargain, but they're rarely worth what you pay. And the practice can become very addictive. They are geared toward impulsive buyers with credit cards, and they can be habit forming very quickly.

• <u>Check your credit rating and fix your credit</u>. You can never purchase a home unless you have good credit. But it is never too late to fix your credit. Get counseling from a reputable non-profit group that specializes in helping

• <u>Save to buy a home</u>. Owning your own home is the American Dream. It's worth sacrificing a little today so that you and your family can have a better life tomorrow. But in order to buy a home, you'll need a down payment, usually 5-10 percent of the cost of the home. If you think about what you'll need a break it down into weekly increments over a several year period, your dream will look closer than you might imagine.

Homework

• Make a list of exactly what you need, before you go shopping at a mall or department store.

• Share the list with your partner.

• Reach an agreement about what you're going to buy, and make sure it's within your budget.

• Don't purchase anything that is not on the list, no matter how big a sale or how much you want it.

• Write down the things you wanted but didn't buy, and discuss with your partner if these should go on next week's list.

Notes